P9-APO-076

Harry Potter

POSTER BOOK

HOGWARTS
THROUGH THE YEARS

SCHOLASTIC INC.
NEW YORK TORONTO LONDON AUCKLAND SYDNEY
MEXICO CITY NEW DELHI HONG KONG BUENOS AIRES

No part of this publication may be reproduced in whole or in part,
or stored in a retrieval system, or transmitted in any form of by any means,
electronic, mechanical, photocopying, recording, or otherwise,
without written permission of the publisher.
For information regarding permission, write to Scholastic Inc.,
Attention: Permissions Department, 557 Broadway, New York, NY 10012.

ISBN 13: 978-0-439-02490-7
ISBN 10: 0-439-02490-0

Copyright © 2007 by Warner Bros. Entertainment Inc.
HARRY POTTER characters, names, and related indicia are trademarks of and
© Warner Bros. Entertainment Inc.
Harry Potter Publishing Rights © J.K. Rowling.
(s07)
All rights reserved. Published by Scholastic Inc.
SCHOLASTIC and associated logos
are trademarks and/or registered trademarks of Scholastic Inc.

Art Direction by Rick DeMonico
Interior designed by Two Red Shoes Design
Special Thanks to Henry Ng for his design expertise

12 11 10 9 8 7 6 5 4 3 2 1 7 8 9/0

Printed in Mexico
First printing, June 2007

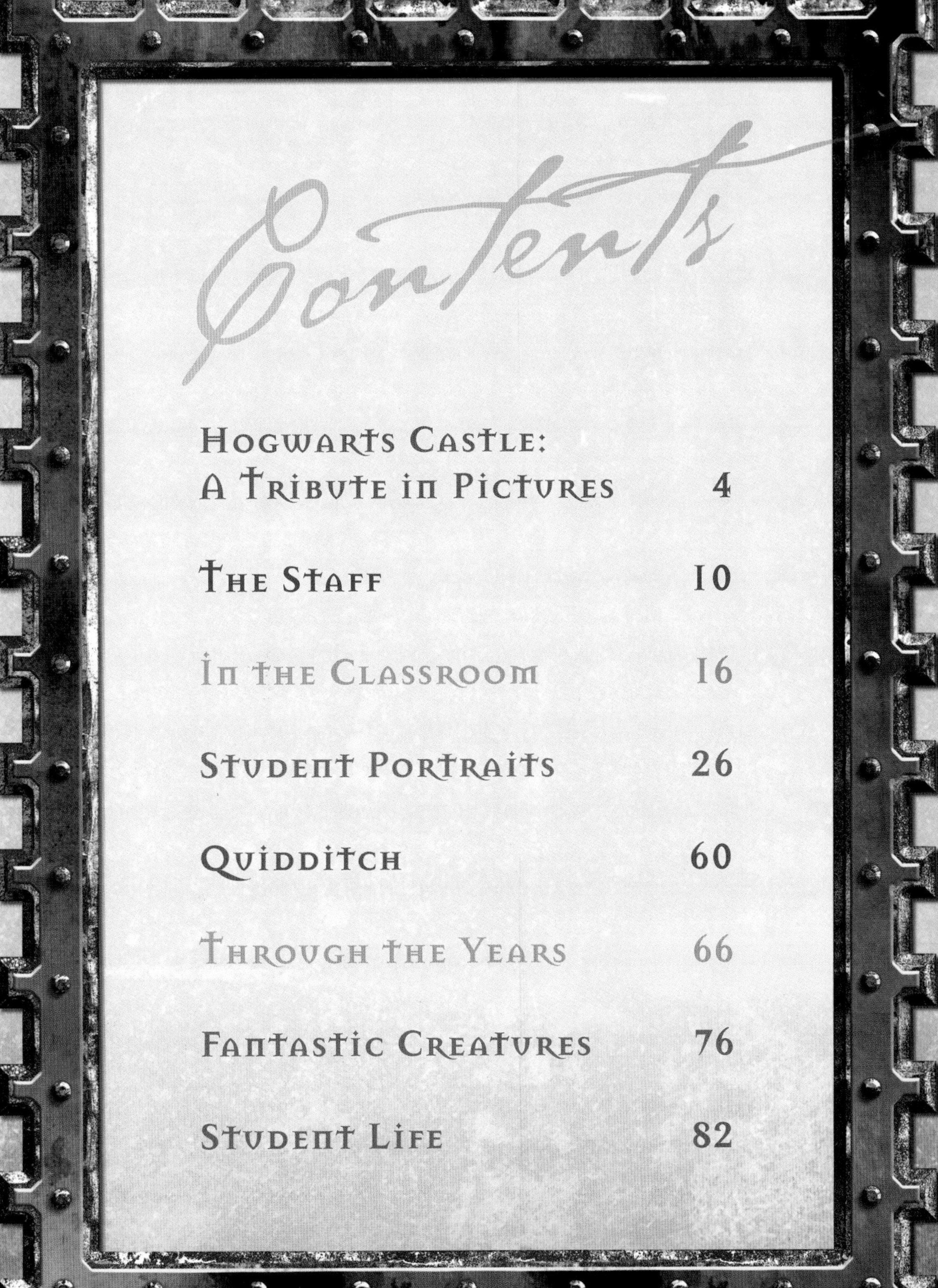

Contents

Hogwarts Castle:
A Tribute in Pictures

HOGSMEADE

The Grounds

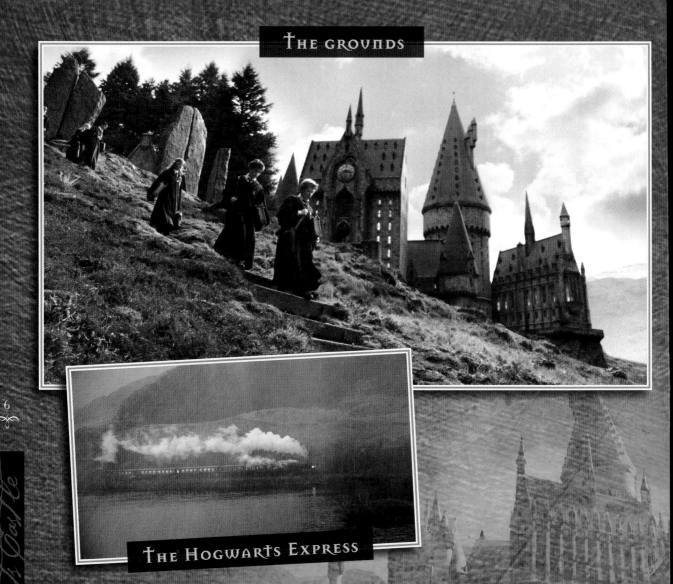

The Hogwarts Express

The Great Hall

The Chamber of Secrets

The Fat Lady — entrance to Gryffindor Tower

The Gryffindor common room

Hogwarts corridors and staircases

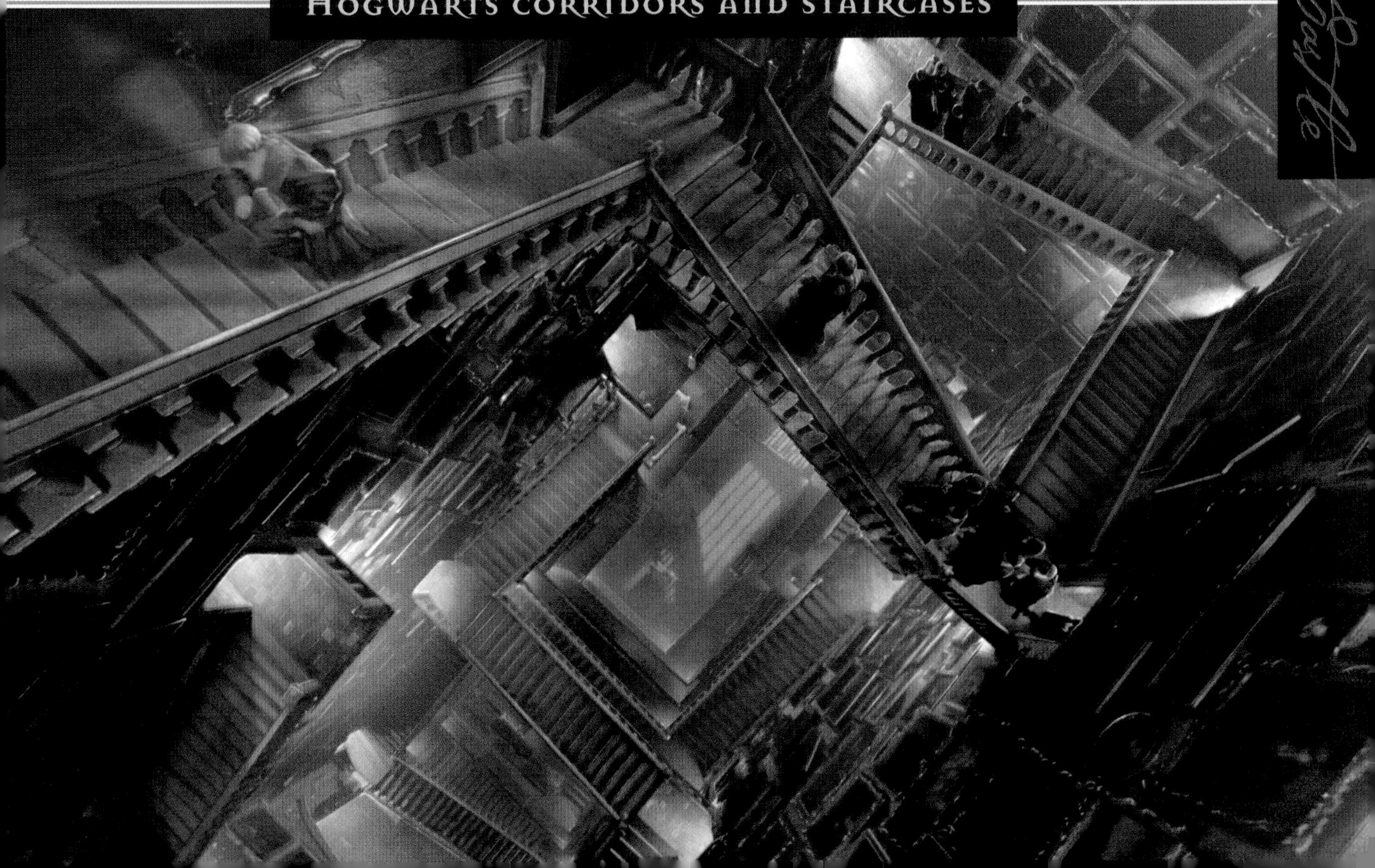

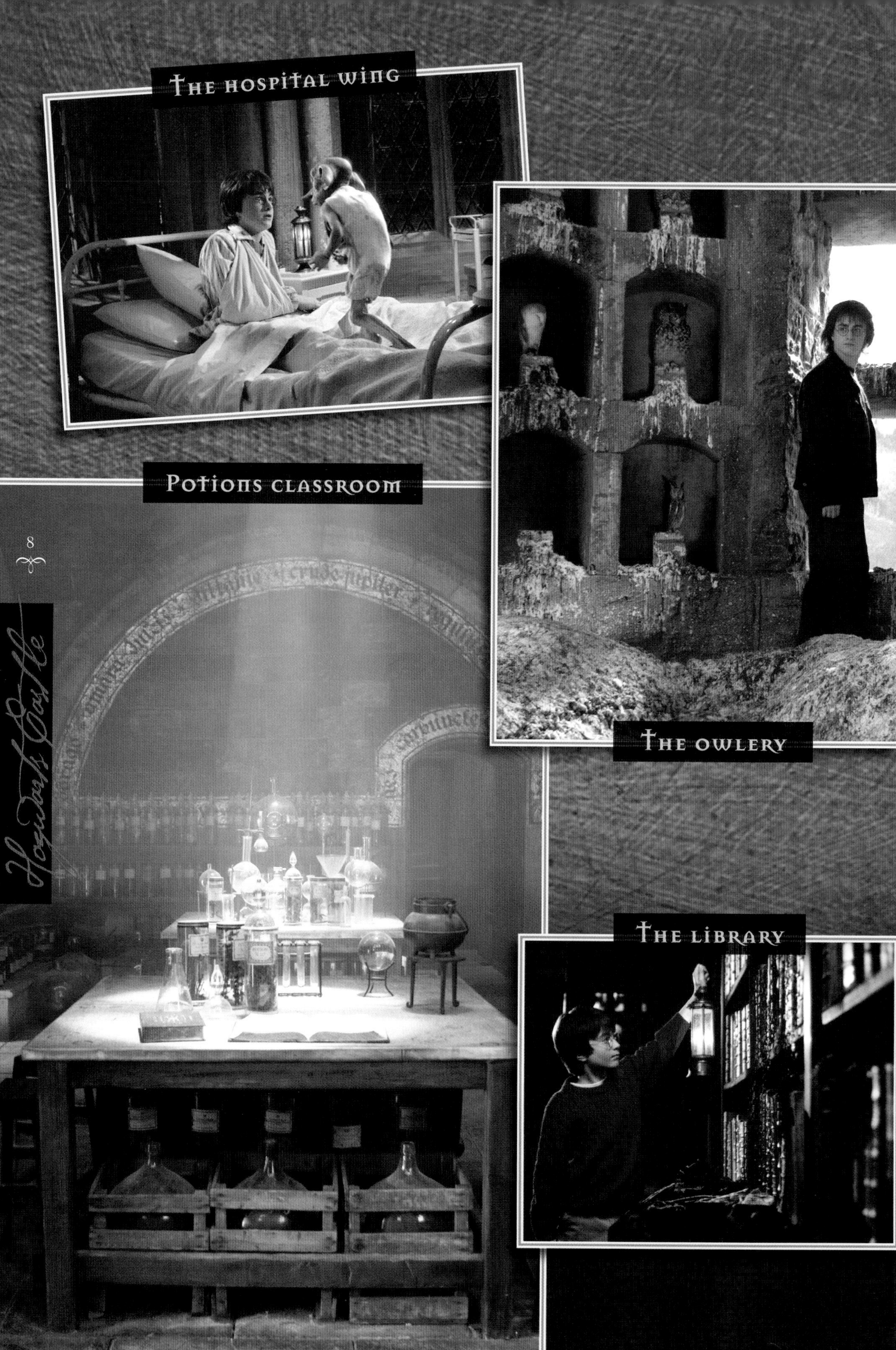

The hospital wing

The owlery

Potions classroom

The library

The Whomping Willow

Hagrid's hut

The Slytherin common room

Hogwarts Castle

The Staff

The Hogwarts Staff

ALBUS DUMBLEDORE
HEADMASTER

Minerva McGonagall
Deputy Headmistress,
Transfiguration teacher,
Head of Gryffindor House

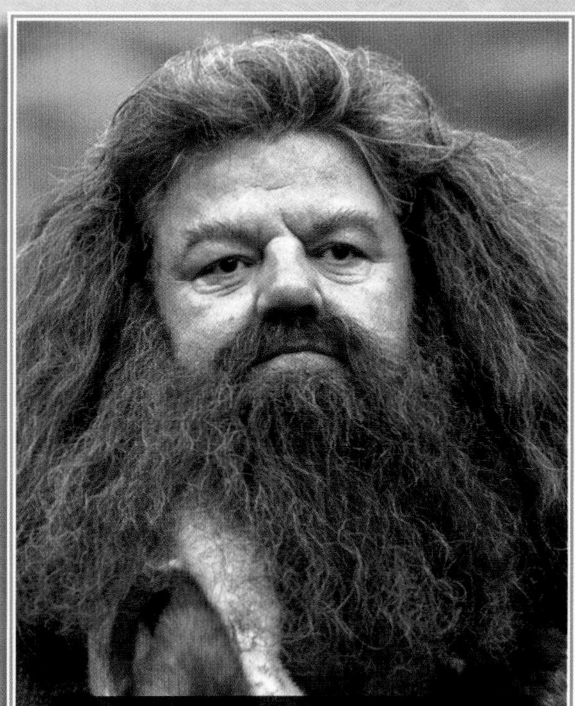

Rubeus Hagrid
Keeper of Keys and Grounds
and Care of Magical
Creatures teacher

Severus Snape
Potions master and
Head of Slytherin House

Filius Flitwick
Charms teacher and
Head of Ravenclaw House

Argus Filch
Caretaker

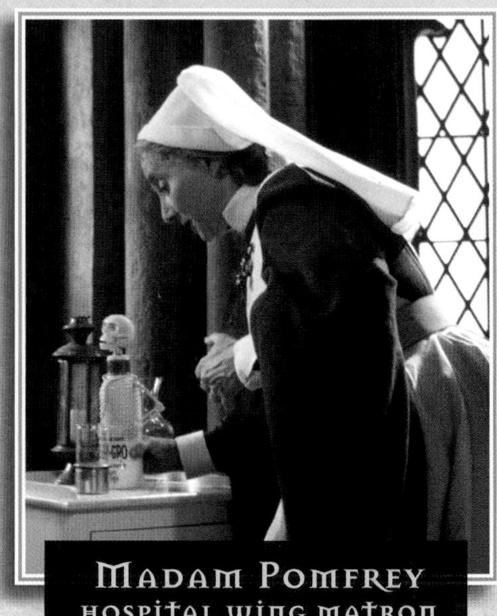
Madam Pomfrey
hospital wing matron

Sibyll Trelawney
Divination teacher

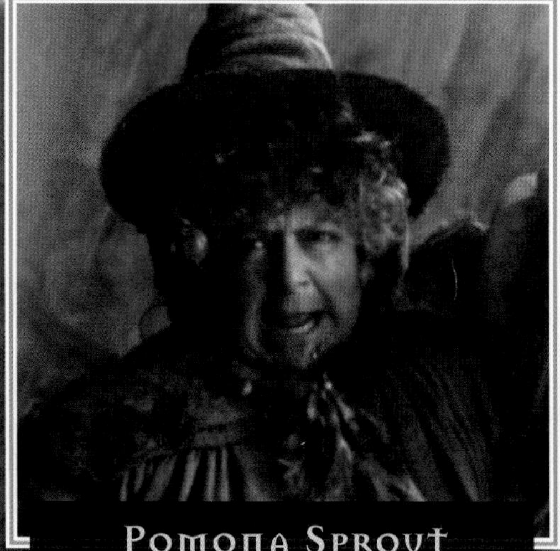
Pomona Sprout
Herbology teacher and
Head of Hufflepuff House

Madam Hooch
Quidditch teacher

Defense Against the Dark Arts Teachers

Quirinus Quirrell
Year One

Gilderoy Lockhart
Year Two

Remus Lupin
Year Three

Alastor "Mad-Eye" Moody
Year Four

Dolores Umbridge
Year Five

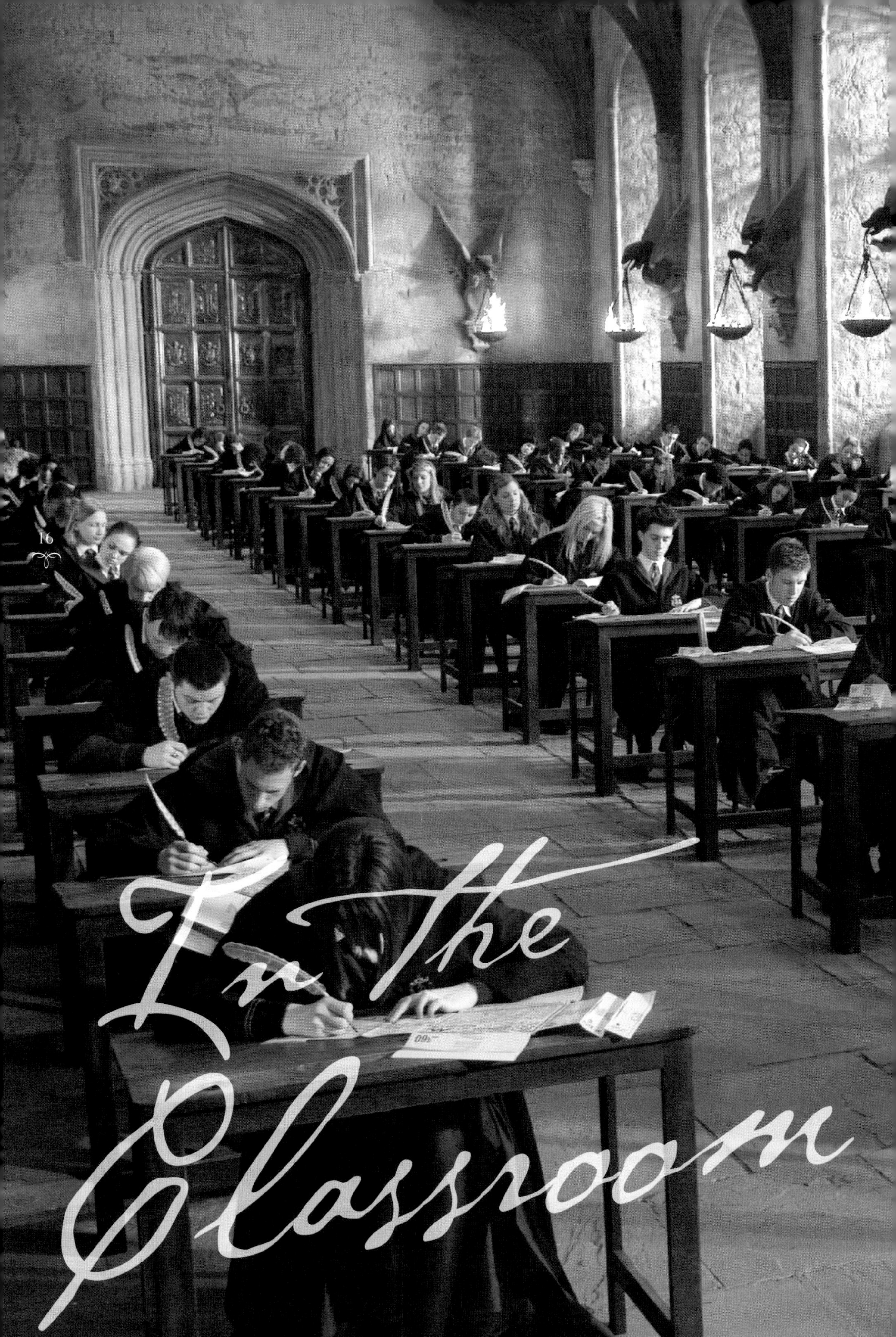

In The Classroom

Year One

Year Two

Year Three

Year Three

Year Four

Year Five
Dumbledore's Army (the "D.A.")

Student Portraits

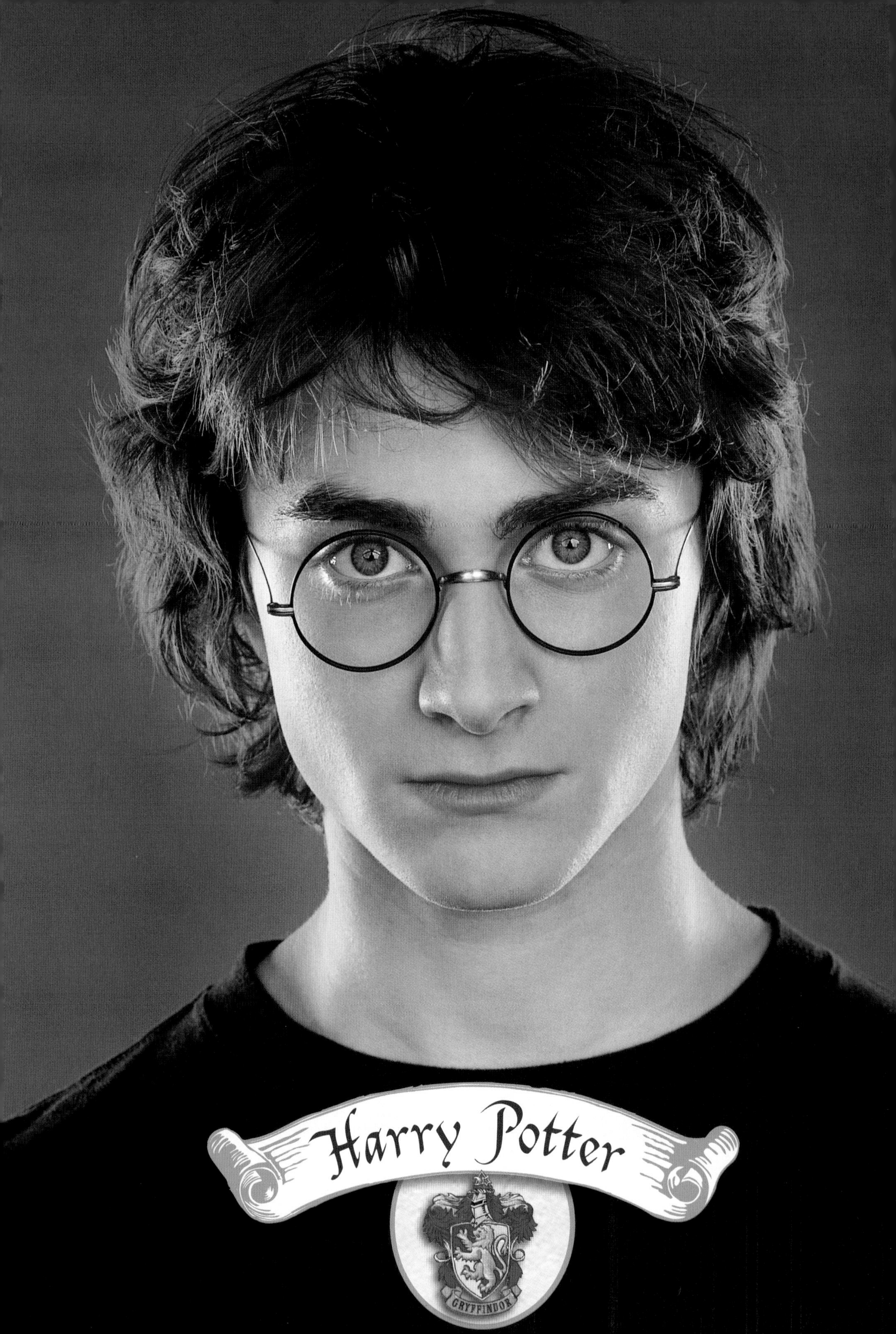
Harry Potter
GRYFFINDOR

Student Portraits

Hermione Granger
GRYFFINDOR

Student Portraits

Ron Weasley
GRYFFINDOR

Student Portraits

Fred and George Weasley
GRYFFINDOR

Student Portraits

Ginny Weasley
GRYFFINDOR

Neville Longbottom
GRYFFINDOR
Student Portraits

Padma Patil

GRYFFINDOR

Parvati Patil

Dean Thomas

Draco Malfoy
SLYTHERIN

Vincent Crabbe
SLYTHERIN
Gregory Goyle
SLYTHERIN

Cedric Diggory
HUFFLEPUFF

Cho Chang

Luna Lovegood
RAVENCLAW
Student Portraits

Quidditch

Through the Years

Year One

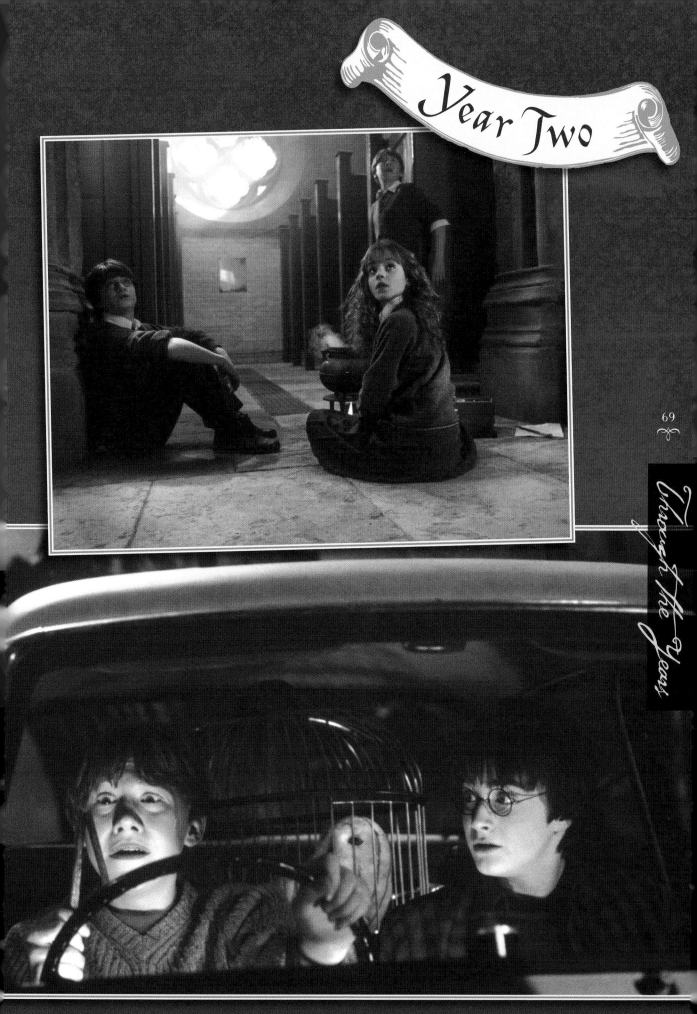

Year Two

Year Three

Year Four

Year Five

Fantastic Creatures

Fawkes the phoenix

Basilisk

Dobby the house-elf

Cornish pixie

A boggart in the form of Professor Snape (Neville's greatest fear), then a giant spider (Ron's greatest fear)

A Hungarian Horntail dragon

Dementor

Sirius Black in Animagus form

Werewolf

Mermaid

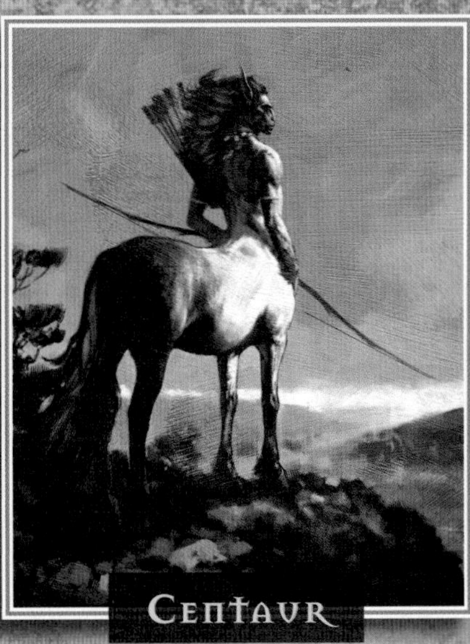
Centaur

Thestral

Buckbeak the Hippogriff

Goblin

Student Life

Student Organizations

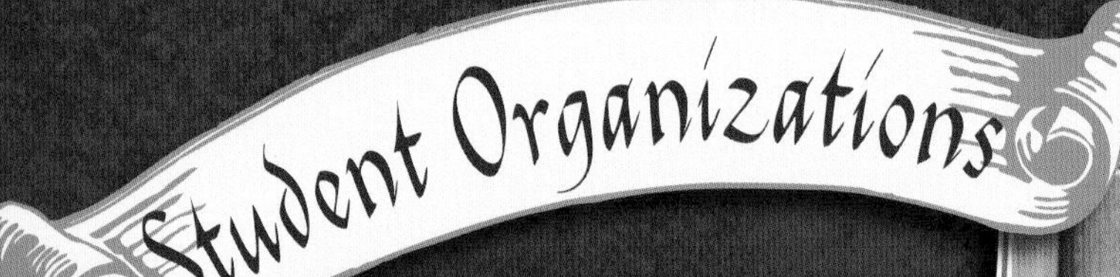

The Dueling Club

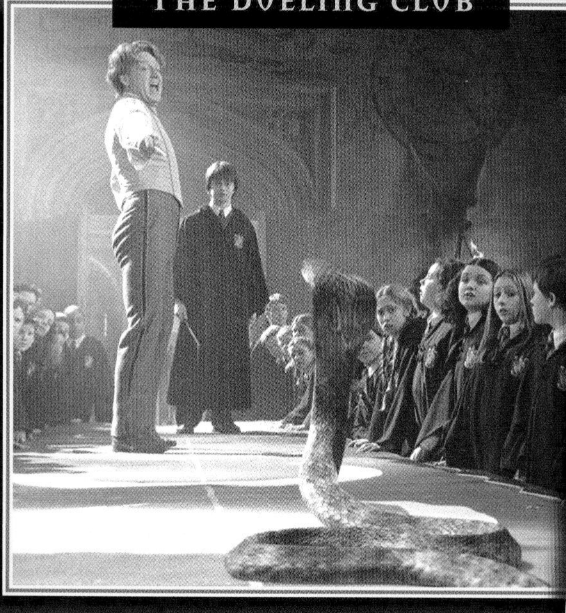

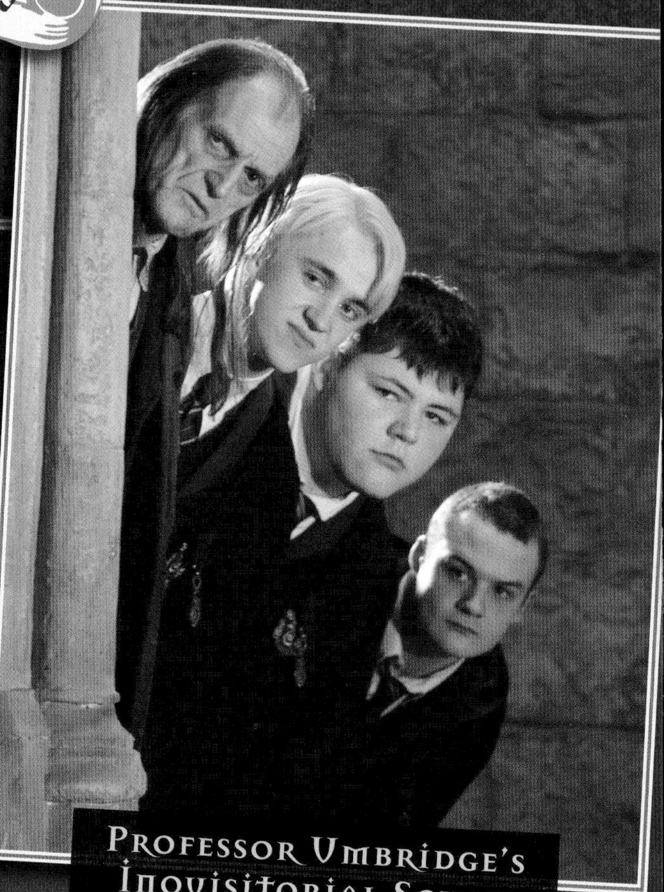

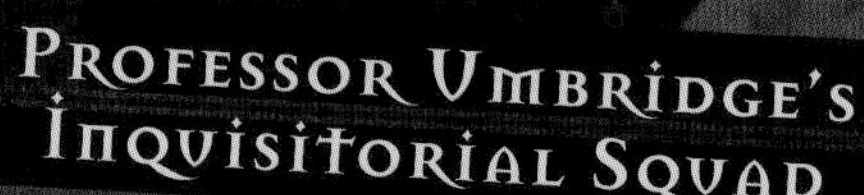

Professor Umbridge's Inquisitorial Squad

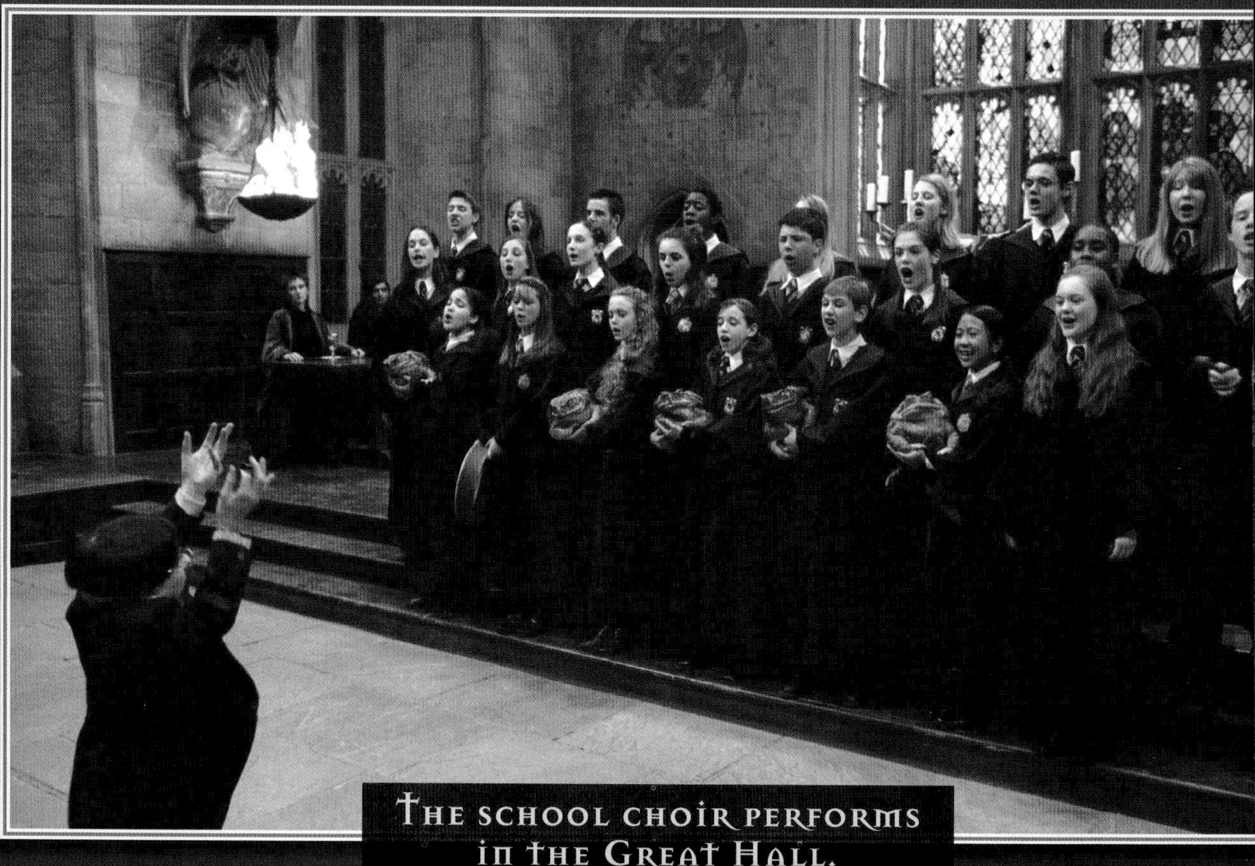

The school choir performs in the Great Hall.

Hogsmeade Weekends

The Triwizard Tournament

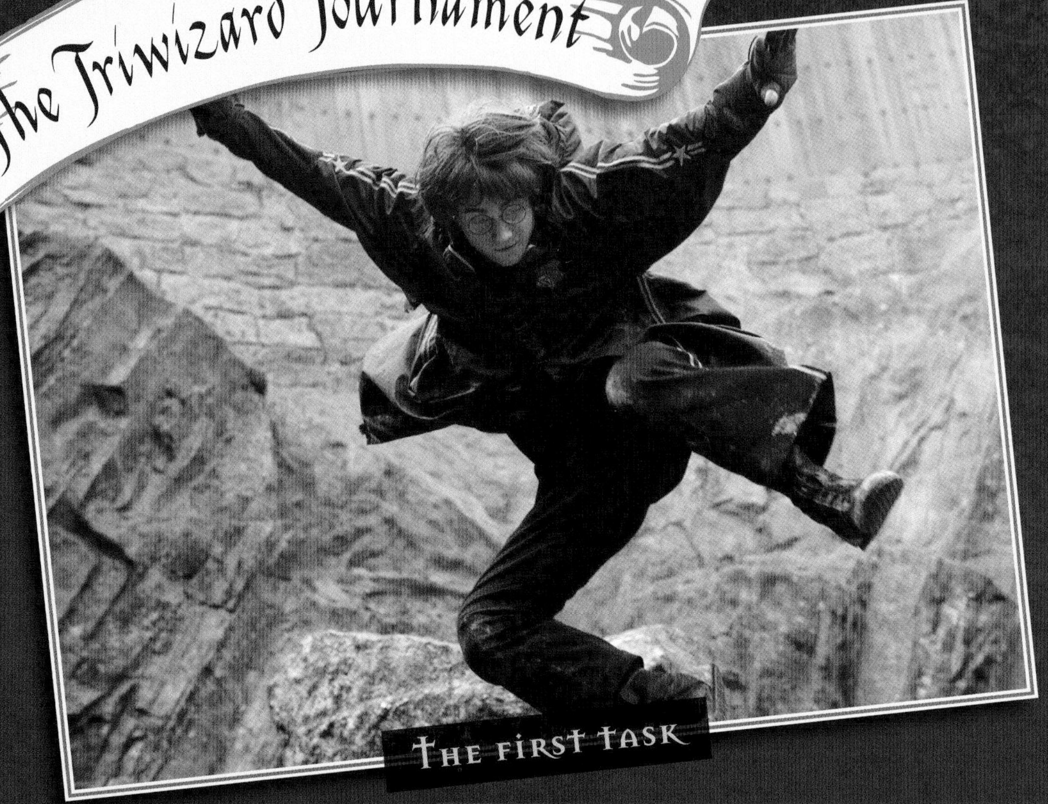

The first task

An important clue to the second task

The Goblet of Fire

After the second task

Durmstrang champion
Viktor Krum

Beauxbatons champion
Fleur Delacour

The third task

Hogwarts champions Harry Potter
and Cedric Diggory

The Yule Ball